Breakfast for Ducklings

by Jeanine Meyer-Gelhaus ✦ *illustrated by Maryn Roos*

SRAonline.com

 SRA

Send all inquiries to this address:
SRA/McGraw-Hill
4400 Easton Commons
Columbus, OH 43219

ISBN: 978-0-07-620914-9
MHID: 0-07-620914-8

1 2 3 4 5 6 7 8 9 PHX 13 12 11 10 09 08

The **McGraw·Hill** Companies

Breakfast for Ducklings

by Jeanine Meyer-Gelhaus ✦ illustrated by Maryn Roos

McGraw Hill SRA

Columbus, OH

Jon and Erin hopped onto the front seat of the old, red truck. Papa Pete turned the key, and the motor started with a **ka-bang.** It creaked and rumbled as it rolled out onto the street. "This truck sounds funny," Erin said to Papa Pete. "I wish we could get a new one!"

"Our truck is just fine," replied Papa Pete. "It sounds funny because it is just waking up from a long night's sleep. Don't you yawn and stretch when you wake up in the morning?" questioned Papa Pete. Erin just shrugged and looked out the window of the old, red truck.

Each day the children rode with their father to the business he owned. It was called the Gelhaus Family Garage. From there, the children would walk to their elementary school, which was only one block farther down the street.

The old, red truck traveled down Allman Street. It bounced across the Black River Bridge and turned the corner to travel down Park Road before arriving at the garage.

On this particular morning, as the red truck sputtered and rumbled through the park, Erin noticed something new. "Look, Daddy! It's a momma duck with babies!" She was bubbling with joy as she pointed to the little family.

Papa Pete pulled the old truck over on Park Road, right near the picnic table. The mother duck quickly gathered up her babies. All seven tried to hide under her wings.

"They are so cute and fluffy!" squealed Erin with excitement. Jon opened the truck door and stepped onto the grass. Erin followed. **"Quack!"** said the mother duck angrily. Erin handed Jon a brown paper bag.

"What are you doing with those lunches I just packed this morning?" questioned Papa Pete.

"Sharing, just sharing," replied Jon as he took the crust off his tuna salad sandwich.

Papa Pete sighed, "Okay, just a little bread for their breakfast."

The momma duck looked at the bread. She then looked at Jon and Erin. Slowly she stretched out her neck, and in a second, she snatched the soft, white bread from the grass.

Erin grabbed her lunch bag and started to open it. "That's your lunch, Erin!" said Papa Pete sternly. "Besides, if we don't get moving, you two will be late for school."

The children hopped back into the old truck. Papa Pete turned the key, the truck started, and soon it was again sputtering and banging its way down Park Road.

The next day, as the old, red truck crossed the Black River Bridge, the children could already see the duck family sitting near the picnic table. They were sitting right where the children had fed them the previous morning.

Erin looked at her dad, and without a word, he smiled and pulled the truck near the picnic table once again. Erin pulled out a whole slice of white bread from under her jacket. Her father looked at her with great surprise. "I was just keeping it warm," she said with a soft grin on her face. "And it is not my lunch. I brought this extra slice for the ducks' breakfast."

She tore the slice into tiny pieces. The momma duck immediately moved towards the bread, and to everyone's surprise, all the little ducklings followed her. With seven hungry mouths to feed, the bread quickly disappeared.

This series of events was repeated day after day. **Bang, clang...** the old, red truck travels down Allman Street, crosses the Black River Bridge, turns down Park Road, and breakfast is served to the duckling family who is sitting there waiting.

One day, Papa Pete's alarm did not go off. The Gelhaus family was running very late. As they headed down Allman Street and across the Black River Bridge, Jon and Erin could already see the duck family heading towards the picnic table where the ducks and children always met. The ducks had heard the sound of the old, red truck as it banged and sputtered across the bridge and they were soon quacking and flapping their wings in anticipation of breakfast.

"Honey, we can't stop today," said Papa Pete to his sad little daughter. "We are going to be really late if we do. I hope you can understand. Just open your window, and wish them a good morning, so they know that we are thinking about them."

So Jon and Erin rolled down their window. They waved and yelled, "Good morning, ducklings! We will see you tomorrow!" The momma duck's head turned and watched the red truck pass by. Then all of the little ducklings' heads moved slowly from side to side as well. The ducks were surprised that the old truck did not stop with their breakfast treat. They walked around the picnic table looking for the bread crumbs, but there were no crumbs to be found.

On the following day, as soon as the ducks heard the sound of the old truck banging and rumbling its way across the Black River Bridge, they were not taking any chances. As the truck turned the corner onto Park Road, the ducks immediately started running towards it. "Look, Dad," said Jon with laughter in his voice. "The ducks are coming to meet us." The ducks ran to the side of the road, and Papa Pete beeped the horn. The ducks quacked back and everyone laughed. The children jumped out of the truck and began to open up their lunch bags. The ducks huddled around the children's feet waiting for their breakfast. Papa Pete smiled as he watched the children and the ducks on the warm spring morning.

And so it went, day after day. The ducks would run to meet the Gelhaus children in the old, red truck each and every morning.

About a week before school was going to be out for the summer, a thunderstorm in the night knocked out the electricity at the Gelhaus home. Once again, the alarm did not go off. Papa Pete stood at the kitchen table making sandwiches for the children's lunches. "Hurry, children, grab your books, jackets, and lunch bags. We are late again," said Papa Pete as he grabbed his jacket and a green baseball hat. When Papa Pete had his back turned, Erin grabbed three extra slices of bread from the plastic bag and put them in her lunch sack. She noticed that the mother duck and her babies were getting bigger and fatter each day. "I think they need more than one slice of bread for breakfast," she whispered to herself as she grabbed her jacket and headed toward the door.

As the truck traveled down Allman Street, across the Black River Bridge, and onto Park Road, Erin took the three slices of bread from her lunch bag. "Can't stop today," sighed Papa Pete. "You kids will be marked tardy at school and my mechanics will all be waiting outside the garage because the doors are locked."

"But Daddy, please? I have a special treat for the ducks today," begged Erin.

"Sorry, little one, but we simply can't stop," replied Papa Pete.

"Bye, ducks. I'm sorry we are late and can't stop," yelled Erin out the window.

The ducks heard her voice drifting in the wind and saw her blonde hair flying from the window. As Erin rolled up the side window, Jon looked out the back window.

"Dad," Jon said with a gasp. "They're following us!"

Sure enough, the ducks were running after the children in the old, red truck. "Well, well," said Papa Pete as he looked in his rearview mirror. "This is not good! They could get hit." Papa Pete slowed down. But then the ducks ran even faster to catch up.

"You've got to lose them before we get to that busy corner up there, Dad," said Jon as he pointed up ahead. "Drive faster!"

Papa Pete stepped on the gas. **Vroom! Bang!** The old, red truck rumbled down Park Road.

This time when Jon looked back, he saw that the ducks were now far in the distance. "They must have slowed down" said Papa Pete. "I'm glad because there is a lot of traffic at our corner this morning."

"I'm sad," sighed Erin. "I'm worried about the ducks." She started to cry.

"They will be fine, Erin," said Jon. "You'll see. Tomorrow they will be waiting for us by the picnic table."

"That's right, Erin," said Papa Pete. "Don't worry." He reached over, giving his little girl a reassuring hug. "Tomorrow the ducks will be waiting for breakfast, just like they are every day!"

Papa Pete pulled up to the Gelhaus Family Garage and opened the four large garage doors. The mechanics began to arrive and soon cars were moving in and out of the building. Jon and Erin hurried down the sidewalk toward their school. Soon everyone was busy working or studying.

About ten minutes later, a mechanic came to Papa Pete's office. "Hey, boss," the man said smiling, "You have got to come and see this." Papa Pete got up from his chair. "What is the matter?" he replied with worry in his voice. The two men walked into the garage where the mechanics were busy working on the cars. To everyone's great surprise, the momma duck and her seven little ducklings were marching right through the Gelhaus Garage. They had entered through the open garage door at the far end of the building. Their necks were stretched out, and their heads were held high in the air. They looked this way and that way as they headed straight towards Papa Pete.

"Well, I never," said Papa Pete as he shook his head in amazement.

The mechanics were also surprised. They put down their tools and watched the little parade. "New employees?" questioned one of the mechanics as he teased Papa Pete. "No, I think they are here to buy a new car!" replied Papa Pete with laughter in his voice.

Suddenly a car started to back up as it was removed from the hoist. **"Look out!"** shouted Papa Pete as he tried to chase the ducks out of the path of the car. The ducks moved off to the side, but when the car passed, they continued on their journey towards Papa Pete.

"A busy garage is no place for a family of ducks!" scolded one of the mechanics with a frown on his face. The ducks sat down in the center of the garage. They looked at Papa Pete. Papa Pete looked at the ducks.

"Now what do I do?" questioned Papa Pete scratching his head.

He went to his office and returned with his brown lunch bag. As soon as he opened the bag, the ducks were on their feet. They headed straight for their breakfast. Papa Pete had an idea. He placed a small crumb of bread on the garage floor. The ducks all raced for the food. He laid another piece of bread down just beyond the first. The ducks followed the bread. Soon Papa Pete had a bread crumb trail that led out the doors and into the morning sun. As soon as the ducks were outside, a mechanic quickly shut the large garage doors to keep them out. Papa Pete heard the mechanic say through the window, "This garage is too dangerous for ducks. No ducks allowed!"

Once outside, Papa Pete made a trail of bread crumbs straight to the small creek that ran along the back edge of the Gelhaus Garage property. The ducks ate and ate, and soon they settled into the soft, green grass for a nap in the sun. Papa Pete went back to work.

At the end of the school day, Jon and Erin walked to the garage to meet their dad. "I'm still worried about my ducks," said Erin as she wrinkled up her face. Papa Pete laughed and said, "I have an interesting story to tell you two!" After telling the children what had happened at the garage earlier, Papa Pete, Jon, and Erin walked to the creek to check on the ducks. Sure enough, the ducks were still there. In fact, the ducks decided to stay there permanently. They liked their new home. It was close to the water, close to the school, and best of all, close to the Gelhaus Garage, which meant fresh bread for breakfast almost every day of the week.

Meet the Author

Jeanine Meyer-Gelhaus

Jeanine Meyer-Gelhaus has traveled all over the world! She traveled to Costa Rica, Russia, Brazil, South Africa, Ireland, and even Japan. The things Jeanine sees, touches, smells, tastes, and hears during her world travels become the inspiration for her writing. When at home in Medford, Wisconsin, Jeanine teaches middle school science, a job that gives her a chance to challenge and encourage young people. She also loves baseball. Jeanine has visited stadiums all across the United States.